Calm at the Restaurant

W9-AON-169

Adapted by Alexandra Cassel Schwartz
Based on the screenplay written by Mary Jacobson
Poses and layouts by Jason Fruchter

SIMON SPOTLIGHT

An imprint of Simon & Schuster Children's Publishing Division • New York London Toronto Sydney New Delhi
1230 Avenue of the Americas, New York, New York 10020
This Simon Spotlight paperback edition August 2019
For information about special discounts for bulk purchases, please contact Simon & Schuster Special Sales at
1-866-506-1949 or business@simonandschuster.com. • Manufactured in the United States of America 0719 LAK
1 2 3 4 5 6 7 8 9 10 • ISBN 978-1-5344-5193-3 (pbk) • ISBN 978-1-5344-5194-0 (eBook)

It was a beautiful night in the neighborhood, and the Tiger family was doing something special for dinner.

"We're going to meet our friend Jodi Platypus at the neighborhood restaurant!" Daniel said.

Daniel was so excited, he could barely sit still!

Daniel sang and danced around the yard as they waited for Trolley. "Restaurant, restaurant, res-tau-rant!" he cheered. He was feeling silly.

When Trolley arrived, Daniel climbed aboard and even danced on his seat! He kept cheering, "Restaurant, restaurant, res-tau-rant!"

"I know you're excited," said Dad Tiger, "but there are times to be silly and times to be calm. Right now we need to be calm so we can ride safely on Trolley." Dad helped Daniel calm down by singing,

♪ *"Give a squeeze, nice and slow,* ♪
♪ *take a deep breath and let it go."* ♪

Daniel squeezed his sillies out, and when he felt calm, he buckled his seat belt, and Trolley was able to start moving.

When Trolley pulled up on Main Street, the Tiger family hopped off and walked toward the restaurant.

"Since we're not on Trolley anymore, can we be silly now?" Daniel wondered.

Mom and Dad thought that was a grr-ific idea. They all sang and danced their way down the sidewalk!

But when they arrived at the quiet restaurant, Daniel knew it was time to be calm again. He sang,

♪ *"Give a squeeze, nice and slow,* ♪
♫ *take a deep breath and let it go."* ♪

Then he took a great big breath in and out. That made him feel more calm.

Jodi and her mom were already at the restaurant when Daniel's family arrived. Prince Tuesday showed the Tigers over to their table and handed everyone a menu. "I hope you are all royally excited, because tonight is . . . taco night!" Prince Tuesday said.

"Tigertastic!" said Daniel.

"Yippy Skippy!" said Jodi.

They were both so excited for taco night.

"I'm going to make the biggest taco ever," said Jodi. She sang loudly and wiggled in her chair.

♪ *"Crunchy shell and juicy tomatoes!"* ♪

Daniel joined in on the fun, singing,

♪ *"Stringy cheese and lots of lettuce!"* ♪

Daniel and Jodi bounced in their seats excitedly.

"Whoa!" said Prince Tuesday, who was right behind them and carrying a tray of food. "Careful there, kiddos."

Daniel was being so silly, he accidentally knocked into Prince Tuesday's tray.

"Daniel," said Mom Tiger, "we are in a restaurant, and that means it's time to be calm."

"You too, Jodi," said Dr. Plat.

Daniel showed Jodi how to calm down while they waited for their food. They sang,

♪ *"Give a squeeze, nice and slow,* ♪
♫ *take a deep breath and let it go."* ♫

Daniel and Jodi both felt calm. "But it's still very hard to wait," said Jodi.

"Maybe we can pretend while we wait," said Daniel. He imagined that there were tacos . . . everywhere!

A taco for you, a taco for me!
My taco world is the place to be.
I love tacos with shredded lettuce and stringy cheese!
From my wonderful taco world!
I'll build my taco way up high
Built with toppings from the sky!
I love tacos with sour cream and juicy tomatoes!
From my wonderful taco world.
My taco world is the place to be.
Tacos for you and me!

Imagining made the waiting go by quickly. Prince Tuesday returned with lots of yummy taco shells and toppings.

"Now we can put whatever we want in our tacos," said Daniel.

Jodi put lots of cheese and beans in her taco. Daniel added lots of crunchy lettuce and tomatoes.

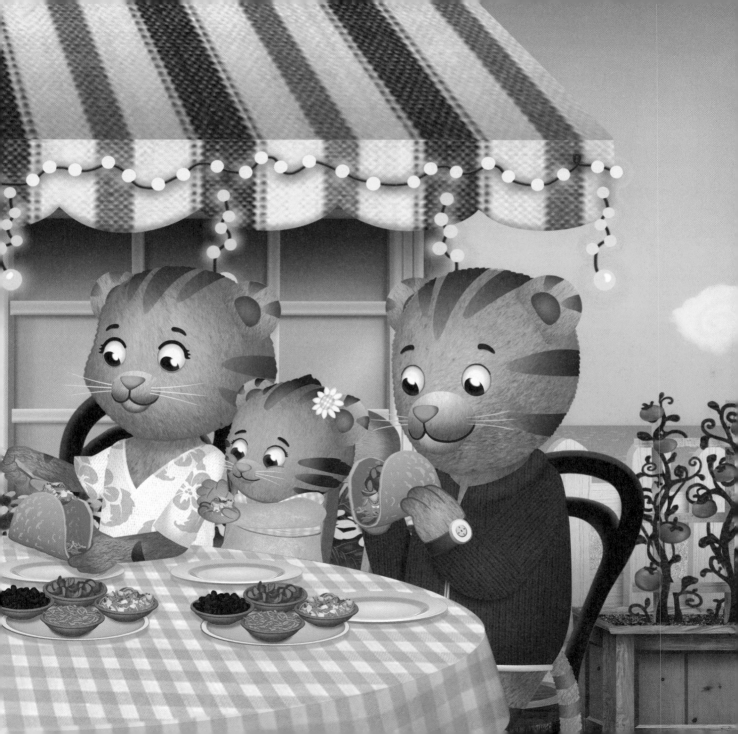

The tacos were delicious! Daniel and Jodi sang,

 *"Tacos for you and tacos for me!"*

But this time they sang very softly and very calmly.
"I like being silly, but it feels good to be calm, too," Daniel
whispered. "Ugga Mugga."

Tigertastic Tic-Tac-Toe

How to play
Tigertastic Tic-Tac-Toe:

One way to stay calm when you go to
a restaurant is to play a game!

To play Tigertastic Tic-Tac-Toe, you'll need two players.
One player uses the X game pieces and the other player uses the
O game pieces. Whoever goes first can put a game piece in any
empty space on the grid. Then the players take turns placing their
X's or O's on the board, trying to get three of their own game pieces
in a row (and trying to keep the other player from getting three of
their game pieces in a row).

The first player to place three of their
game pieces in a row—horizontally,
vertically, or diagonally—wins the
game. If the board is full and no one has
a row of three, it is a tie.

Hope you have a
tigertastic time!